A Note from the Author

John Blue thinks his brother Dane and Dane's friend Lee are sad geeks.

Just because Dane and Lee don't care about how they look. They don't care what anyone thinks about them. Dane and Lee are happy being themselves.

I think that's the best way to be in life. I wish more young people felt they could be like that too. But it's hard sometimes.

I have a soft spot for people like Dane and Lee. I hope you do too by the end of the story.

After all, they are not as daft as they look ...

To Leo,
Sorry about Gabe

Thank you, Thomas and Mark,
for the *Star Wars* fix

Contents

Chapter 1
The Two Cheeses

This story started on a Saturday night when the Two Cheeses hid the telly remote control from me.

Again.

The Two Cheeses?

Maybe you're thinking, *Who are they?* Well, I'll tell you all about them now and get it over with. It has to be done. The Two

Cheeses are a big – a VERY big part of this story.

So, here goes.

The Two Cheeses are the world's saddest geeks.

Fact.

Cheese One is Dane. He's my older brother. Dane's eighteen, I think. But I don't care what age he is. I want *nothing* to do with Dane. See me? I'm normal John Blue. Sixteen. Scottish. Keen on music and girls in that order. I pretend Dane's birthdays just don't happen. Why would I want to party because Dane's been around to stink out my life for another year? He's a greasy, spotty Geek of Geeks. And I'm not being mean, by the way. Dane knows he's greasy and spotty and stinky. He's tall as a lamp post. Thin as a slice of cheese. Dane knows he's a geek, too.

And he's not just any old geek. Dane's a *Star Wars* Geek. Does it bug him like it bugs me? No.

Dane likes being who he is.

Dane doesn't think the way you look or smell matters at all.

"It's what's inside your head that matters. Not what's going on outside it. And, I'm telling you, there's plenty of ace stuff going on in *my* head. Leave me alone," Dane says when me or my mum try to sort him out with zit cream.

"And thanks, but no, thanks, this stuff gunks up your skin. It's normal to sweat," Dane says if we slip XTRA XTRA strong body spray in his room. Hint. Hint.

When we leave shampoo for ultra-greasy hair in the shower, Dane never uses it.

Shampoo strips the hair of its oils, Dane thinks.

So he never uses any of the stuff we buy him. He almost never has a shower anyway.

"I've way too much to do. I can't waste time in the bathroom like the rest of this family," he tuts. As if me and my mum and my dad are the ones with problems! But we're not. And all *he* spends his time doing is being a *Star Wars* Geek. And – oh, yeah! – Dane *does* have problems.

Dane is greasy. VERY. His face and his nose are so slick and shiny that tiny insects could use his face as a Slippy Slide ... *wheeee!* if it wasn't so bumpy with ...

Big.

Red.

Spots.

Lots

And

Lots

And

Lots

Of

Big.

Red.

Spots.

Dane is *covered* with them – his cheeks, his chin, his neck.

"*Here a zit, there a zit, everywhere a zit-zit,*" I sing to him to the tune of 'Old MacDonald Had a Farm'. I'm only telling the truth. And I only get away with slagging Dane like that because I'm one of these buff kind of guys. I was born with perfect skin, and I like to look after it with deep-pore scrubs and plenty of Nivea cream. So I *can* slag Dane. And I do. Well, even Dane's spots have spots ... Not that I ever look at him up close if I can help it. I keep away. Can you blame me? Dane makes me feel sick to my six-pack. And not just because of how he looks.

Because Dane honks.

Fact. Again. Sorry, but my big brother stinks.

Of what?

Well, I don't call him 'Danish Blue' for nothing. I call Dane 'Danish Blue' because he honks like that rank, pongy blue cheese with the blue lines in it. This cheesy smell comes off him. I'm not sure if it comes from his breath, or his underarms, or his feet. I just know it swirls round him.

Pong. Ming. Niff.

So there's Danish Blue. He's one Cheese.

The other Cheese is Dane's mate from college. He's Lee. Poor wee Lee. Another *Star Wars* Geek. Half as tall as Dane. Twice as wide, like God thumped him on the top of his head when he was made. Then squashed him down a bit for a laugh. Kids in school used to call Lee R2-D2. Can you see why?

Now Lee's only half as spotty as Dane, but twice as greasy. Lee's hair always looks as if it's just been washed and it's dripping wet.

Only it hasn't.

And it isn't.

It's just dripping with grease.

I call Lee 'Dairy Lee', because he honks too. He honks like a lump of sweaty cheddar that's been left too long in clingfilm at the back of the fridge. You know that smell? It's bad, isn't it?

Dairy Lee's problem smell seems to come from the bottom. No, not his *bum* – no way would I *ever* go close enough to sniff *that* – but from the bottom part of his body. His feet. Dairy Lee's got foot-fungus. It makes his normal sweat stink like sour milk or old butter. The smell's so bad I just *know* when Dairy Lee's in our house. I know he's there even when I'm up in my room. With the door shut and my mind on important things. I like to spend *my* time doing important things like drumming. Or strumming. Or blasting some sounds. Loud. Or taking a phone call from some babe or other. Even when I'm doing one of these things, I know Dairy Lee's In Da House. So I know when I go down into the sitting room, I'll see the back of Dairy Lee's greasy head.

He'll be sat on the sofa.

Next to Dane.

Both of them will be munching their way through big packets of Outer Space cheese and onion snack-bites.

That's how the Two Cheeses spend every second of their spare time. Side by side. On the sofa. In front of the telly. Scoffing Outer Space snack-bites.

Did you notice that I said, "In front of the telly"?

I didn't say, "Watching the telly."

No. Because the Two Cheeses never watch *normal* telly unless a *Star Wars* film or some show about *Star Wars* is on. They don't watch soaps. Or music shows. Or *The Simpsons*. They only watch *Star Wars* stuff. Nothing else.

Side by side, hour after hour, Dane and Lee sit on the sofa goggling *Star Wars* DVDs.

Or DVDs about the making of *Star Wars.*

Or DVDs about other *Star Wars* fans who goggle *Star Wars* DVDs about the making of *Star Wars* ...

They chant along with their DVDs. They know all the words. They can do all the silly bleeps and sounds of the robots and aliens and spaceships in all the films. They hum and sing along to all the *Star Wars* music, too –

DA **DAH** ... Dadada **DA DAH**.

Even when I'm in my room with my music loud or my amp turned full, I can hear the Two Cheeses singing along to the *Star Wars* theme tune. It's creepy.

What's more creepy is how the Two Cheeses dress. Dane likes to be Chewy or Yoda or Darth Vader. Maybe because he can hide his zits with a mask. Wee Lee prefers to dress up like he's some big-shot hero – Han Solo or Luke Skywalker.

So there you have it – the Two Cheeses. Two cool guys, eh?

And no. They don't have girlfriends.

When they're not at college learning how to build computers, life for the Two Cheeses is *Star Wars*.

But, hey, now you've met the Two Cheeses, I hope you don't feel sorry for them.

They think life is good.

I'm the one you need to feel sorry for.

Me – John Blue.

I'm the one who has to put up with the Two Cheeses.

And I'm the one who never gets to watch normal telly because they've always hidden the remote.

Chapter 2
The Missing Remote

The remote for the telly was missing that Saturday night. I'd come home after a long day working in Frets. Frets is the guitar shop near our house. I work there at the week-ends. You could say I'm into guitars the way the Two Cheeses are into *Star Wars*. Only I'm no geek. Playing the guitar's *my* thing and I'm good at it too. Very, very good, yeah. On Saturday afternoons Frets is always full of older guys who are *so* not nifty players like me. That doesn't stop them thinking they're Eric Clapton or Angus Young. They come into Frets and try out all the guitars. They have a go at playing 'Stairway to Heaven'. When they're done showing off how magic they SO NOT ARE it's my job to re-tune the guitars. Then I polish them up. I have to check they're not broken. I love doing that. I get to play all the guitars in the shop. But it's hard work, too.

The Saturday I started telling you about, I'd been changing broken strings all day. When I came home I was dead beat.

Right, I thought. *I'll slump in front of Kerrang! for an hour. Then shower. Change. Go get me some girl action with my mates.*

Wrong.

See, the Two Cheeses were already plonked in front of the telly. They'd been there all day.

"OK, where's the remote, Dane? Give," I said, patting about my chair so I could switch over from the news.

"Puh. Listen to Little Boy Blue. I knew you'd march in here and take over." Dane sniffed at me. He was wearing his Darth Vader mask. He sounded like he was blowing snot through a megaphone.

Little Boy Blue, I thought. I hate when Dane calls me that.

Dane nudged Lee, who was togged up as a Jedi, with a light sabre and a long cloak. He was reading one of the *Star Wars* fan mags he always carries around.

"Lee, didn't I say Little Boy Blue'd come strutting in and spoil our night?" Dane tutted. He poked his Darth Vader glove in my face. "You're not watching your stupid shouty music shows just because Mum and Dad are out," Dane went on. "They said if you bossed me and Lee, you'd be in trouble. So leave us alone. We're gonna put on *The Empire Strikes Back* and you can't stop us."

"Yeah. See – we were here first, kiddo." Lee spat cheese and onion snack-bites all over my best Guns'n'Roses T-shirt.

"Who you calling kiddo?" I said, brushing gunk off my front. Lee looked hard at me and slid his hand to the button on his plastic light sabre as if he was giving me a warning – *I'll put the Force on you, John Blue.*

Then he went back to his snack-bites and the mag on his knee. I spotted Princess Leia (only decent thing about *Star Wars*). Pwoa! All she wore was her teeny, weeny bikini. And she was smiling up at me like she liked what she was seeing. Lee flicked to the next page.

"You're not even watching the telly. You're reading your sad mag, you loser," I told Lee. I grabbed his Outer Space packet to check if the remote was in there. It was there last time he hid it. Made it almost as greasy as his hair.

No luck.

So I stuck my arm down the back of the sofa right where Lee was sitting. I felt around a bit. Pat, pat, pat. Feel, feel, feel. Suddenly Lee jumped up and yelled, “Dane!” I thought for a horrible moment the warm, squashy thing I’d groped was his warm, squashy butt.

Lucky for both of us it was just a cushion. And lucky it wasn’t me that had made Lee yell. It was something he’d seen in his mag.

“Dane!” Lee yelled again. He’d switched on his light sabre and he was tapping it on the *Star Wars* mag. “Read that, Dane,” Lee went on. “Does this say what I think it says?”

Dane didn’t take off his Darth Vader mask when he read the words Lee was tapping.

That meant Dane's voice came out all deep and thick and Darth Vader-y ...

"STAR WARS FANS OF THE WORLD UNITE!!!

BIGGEST MEETING IN THE HISTORY OF THE GALAXY.

NEW YORK CITY.

PRIZES.

STARS.

JEDI TRAINING.

GALA DINNER.

COSTUME PARTIES.

BE THERE!

AND MAY THE FORCE BE WITH YOU ..."

"Oh. My. God."

Dane fell back on to the sofa when he stopped reading. He was breathing hard through his plastic mask. The big padded shoulders of his black cloak were going up and down with excitement. It was ages before he said anything else. He just shook his head. Panting. At last he said –

"Lee. We. Have. To. Go. To. New. York."

"I know," said Lee. He plopped down next to Dane.

"Fans like us, Lee," Dane nodded.

"Thousands of us, Dane," said Lee.

"Count us in, eh?" said Dane.

"Too right." Lee gave Dane a high five.

Too sad for words, I thought.

"So what do we do?" said Dane.

"Just fill in this form. Send the money. Easy," Lee said with a shrug.

"What's it cost?" asked Dane.

"Only £500 if we book now," said Lee.

"Each?" That was me asking. I laughed out loud.

Lee was nodding like everything was cool.

"It's only £500 with my Gold fan club discount," Lee told Dane proudly. "Gets you money off loads of things. Stickers and socks and pants and –"

"And where are you going to get £500? Outer space?" I asked. I'd bent down onto the floor now. I was poking about for the remote under the sofa. On the telly Graham Norton was prancing about with Carol Smillie. It was more than I could bear.

"Look, where have you put the bloody remote control, ya losers?" I growled at Dane and Lee. As I spoke I rammed my thumb and my index finger up onto my head. It made an **L** shape. **L** for **LOSER**. The two Cheeses HATE it when I chant **L-L-L-LOSER L-L-L-LOSER** like that at them. They go all sniffy and hurt. "We're not losers," they bleat, "We're just different from you."

But did it bother them tonight that I called them **L-L-L-LOSER**?

Not a bit.

I don't think they even *saw* what I was doing. The Two Cheeses were way, way, *way* more upset about something else.

"Little Boy Blue's onto something, Dane." Lee tutted. "Where we gonna find £500? I'm skint."

"I'm always skint." Dane was looking down at his Darth Vader outfit. Was it his outfit's fault it cost £100 of his student loan?

"Would our folks give us some dosh? Nah." Lee shook his head even as he asked himself the question. Dane agreed.

"No chance," he told Lee. "Mum seems to think I waste too much money on *Star Wars* already."

"Really?" I blinked at Dane. Then I said in a helpful way, "You could sell your *Star Wars* action figures."

"You're evil, Little Boy Blue," Dane gasped as if I'd asked him to eat his own hand.

I pointed at Lee.

"Or you could punt your *Star Wars* Lego on eBay? Raise money that way."

"Think you're funny? We *play* with them," Lee gulped at me as if I'd told him to throw himself out the window.

"Well, you better earn some cash. Like I do," I snapped. I was getting bored talking to the Two Cheeses about something they'd never do. Earn some money? Take themselves to New York? They couldn't even take themselves off for a bath.

I went back to look for the remote. I was getting desperate.

Will Young and Cilla Black had joined Graham and Carol on the telly now. They were all singing 'Over the Rainbow'. Staring into each other's eyes. It was horrible. I started bashing the Sky box, trying to change channels by force. Not *The Force*. Just force.

Behind me, Dane and Lee were still going on and on and on about getting money for New York.

"We're *far* too busy to get jobs, Lee," Dane was moaning.

"I know, Dane. But this *Star Wars* meeting is life or death. We need big money," said Lee.

"Yeah," said Dane. "Look. We'll think better if we watch *The Empire Strikes Back*."

"So I'll press to play?" nodded Lee.

Out the corner of my eye I noticed him fumbling up his trouser leg.

"You skanky minger," I shouted.

Can you guess why?

Dairy Lee'd had the missing remote all the time. Now he was pulling it out of his sock. He wiped it dry on his Jedi robe. I dived over and tried to grab the remote before Lee could put on his film.

Yuk!

It was slippy with Lee's sweat. So it shot out of my hand. Slid across the room.

"Little Boy Blue, you are a pain," Dane yelled at me. He put his Darth Vader boot out to stop the remote. He must have pushed up the volume at the same time, because a jolly BBC voice drowned him out:

"Hey! Can YOU sing or dance? Well, why are you sitting at home? Phone in NOW and

you could be here next week to win £10,000 on our brand new talent show …"

The BBC voice was so loud and excited, I had to quit rugby-tackling Dane to put my hands over my ears.

The Two Cheeses were doing the same.

"Turn it down," we mouthed at each other. We were all trying to get hold of the remote.

And then the music started –

DA **DAH …** Dadada **DA DAH …**

Chapter 3
Star Wars

Dane and Lee were frozen to the spot.

"*Star Wars*," they whispered to each other. They were staring at the telly like they were in a trance.

"Not again," I groaned.

I beeped the sound down a bit.

Dane was pointing at the screen. "I didn't know it was on," he whispered.

"It's magic." Lee's eyes were closed. He was swaying to and fro in time to the *Star Wars* theme. Humming along. There was a look of pure joy on his face. He looked very funny but also very sad. I put him right.

"It's not bloody *Star Wars.* It's a stupid show where saddos make prats of themselves," I said. "And we've got another hour of Mr Saturday Night – that pie, Jack Gloss." I groaned as an orange face winked at me from the TV. I pointed the remote at the telly.

"Don't you dare," Dane hissed.

"You must not," Lee warned.

Dane and Lee closed in on me. They grabbed my arms – one each. Scary. How could two geeks be so strong?

"I think we must watch this," Dane told Lee in a deep Darth Vader-y way. He was nodding at the screen. It was flashing a message –

Star Wars.

Win £10,000.

Call now!

Star Wars.

Win £10,000.

Call now!

There was a phone number across the bottom of the screen. Jack Gloss was grinning with his too-white teeth and pointing out at me and the Two Cheeses. He was telling us to get on the phone, ring the *Star Wars* number and come on down to London next week to win.

"I'd rather pole dance in a prison than come on down to meet you," I muttered at the telly. I grinned at the Two Cheeses to see if they liked what I'd said. But they weren't sneering at Jack Gloss like I was. No. They were nodding at him like he was Yoda.

"Hey, Lee," asked Dane. "You thinking what I'm thinking?"

"I'm thinking I should get on my mobile, Dane," Lee answered. "We should get us on this *Star Wars* show and do our thing. Win us some B-I-I-I-G money for NEW YORK CITY." Lee was yakking all Yankee. His mouth was wide open. I caught a vile guff of his cheesy breath as I broke free of him and Dane.

Oh, man! I couldn't take any more of this. The Two Cheeses had won. Their geekiness had got to me so much that I HAD to escape from them. *Kerrang!* or no *Kerrang!*

But of course, I couldn't leave them to *Star Wars with Mr Saturday Night* without the last word.

As Lee was punching the phone number into his mobile, I shouted, "What the hell can you geeks do on a talent show? Who would vote for you? And what you gonna sing? The

Star Wars soundtrack? **L-L-L-LOSER L-L-L-L-L-L-LOSER,"** I stabbed an **L** to my head and chanted first at Dane. Then at Lee.

I kept on chanting –

"L-L-L-LOSER L-L-L-LOSER"

All the way upstairs.

Chapter 4

L-L-L-LOSER L-L-L-LOSER

I didn't stop when I went into my room.

"**L-L-L-LOSER L-L-L-LOSER**," I sneered as I picked up a guitar. I didn't think about the notes I was chanting. I just played them. In my head I could hear Johnny Rotten singing instead of me. Spitting out my words. Nasty. Angry. Then Joey Ramone. Iggy. Freddie Mercury. Angus Young. Mick Jagger. Elvis.

"**L-L-L-LOSER L-L-L-LOSER**," I could hear them all singing. Different rock gods, and kings of punk. I could hear them all in my head. Singing my *chant.* Making it sound great.

Whoa! All the hairs on my arms stood up. I was onto something. I could feel it in my bones.

So I forgot the Two Cheeses. Forgot I was going out. I ignored the beeping from texts on my mobile.

JB y r u l8? T b xxxx

I wasn't going anywhere tonight. I had work to do.

I turned the notes of **L-L-L-LOSER L-L-L-LOSER** into power chords. Beefed them up. Gave them some welly. Turned my insult into a riff. It was mean and hard. I liked it. Couldn't get it out of my head –

L-L-L-LOSER L-L-L-LOSER

Then I worked out a keyboard part while I still had the riff in my mind. **Jab.Jab.Jab** it went, like a drill in your skull. I added some bass. A drum lick. Then I thought I'd better write down all the parts. Fast. Before I forgot them. I thought I'd better record them too. It wasn't every day a hook like this popped into my head. Mostly when I wrote songs with the mates in my band we'd take weeks. We'd fight over every note and change them all. Over and over. We'd fall out about the songs we wrote.

But *this* hook, the one I'd sung at the Two Cheeses – and this isn't boasting. Hey, I'm not a boastful guy at all – *this* hook felt like a *classic*. An anthem. The sort of thing thousands of people could shout at a massive rock gig. Feet stomping. Fists punching the air ...

L-L-L-LOSER L-L-L-LOSER

I worked on my idea for hours. My folks came home from whatever they'd been doing. They read the KEEP OUT notice on my door and called, "Goodnight, son," and went to bed. Some time later I heard Dane letting Lee out the front door.

"May the force be with you," Dane boomed.

"And also with you," Lee answered. I heard his scooter crunching up our garden path. His scooter, by the way, is not one you ride on the road. Just in case you're thinking Lee is some sort of biker-dude in leathers. No, Lee's scooter is the fold-up kind you push along with your foot. Lee shouted out something else to Dane before he scooted home in his Jedi robe.

"Our song rocks! New York, here we come."

I was too busy thinking up the words for **L-L-L-LOSER L-L-L-LOSER** to care what Lee was talking about. Just wished he'd shut up and go home.

But a week later I got a massive shock. It was even worse than if I ever happen to see Dane's spotty back ...

Chapter 5
Total

Sorry, but I can't tell you about this **SHOCK!!!!!!!!** right now. First you have to understand how much *hassle* I had trying to finish my **L-L-L-LOSER** song.

The morning after I wrote the **L-L-L-LOSER** hook, I rang the three guys in my band, Total.

"Dudes, we *have* to jam," I told them. "I've written the best riff ever."

Plunk, the bass player, was not happy that I'd rung him first thing on a Sunday. If I told you what he called me and my **L-L-L-LOSER** riff, this story would have an X-rated sticker on it. So I better not. Anyway, Plunk didn't want to jam. But he never does. He says Total play too loud.

Stonk the drummer showed up. Me and Stonk and Stonk's drums went along to Matt's house.

"Things are looking good," I told Stonk on the way. "Me on guitar, you on drums, Matt on lead vocals. That's three out of four band members in the same place at the same time. We're rocking, dude."

I need to explain here that Total have only ever played as a total band once.

That was our first and only gig. We were booed off stage.

Called Total Crap.

Total Pish.

Total Mince ... and worse.

Our music career's kind of been on hold ever since.

Matt was still in bed when we got to his house. But he said we could jam in his room. The jam was Total Crap. I blame Matt. He was there in the room but he wasn't really *there*. Not in spirit. He'd been chucked by his girlfriend so he was all mopey and lovesick. And he wouldn't get out of bed. Kept ducking under his duvet to send his ex texts instead of helping me write words.

Listen to Matt's best effort after six hours –

My heart is dead

Coz my girl, she said

Don't wanna see you any more

How can I

L-L-L-LOSE HER?

Don't wanna

L-L-L-LOSE HER.

Matt thought he'd done top work, turning my punky riff into a love song.

"No," I told Matt. "That's crap. You've fitted your own soppy words into that soppy song I hate. *"You're Beautiful ..."* I sang in a high girly voice.

Matt took that as massive compliment. He texted his words to his ex. Then went round to sing them to her. Left me with Stonk.

Stonk really loved my **L-L-L-LOSER** riff. He made me cart the drums back to his house so we could carry on playing.

"This is *evil*," Stonk hissed at me while he thumped out **L-L-L-LOSER**.

I played along on guitar and sang it. Trouble is, he thumped **L-L-L-LOSER** out and wouldn't stop. Just drummed faster. Louder. Wilder. He roared at me to keep up with him. I did my best till my fingers started bleeding.

"Can we write verses now?" I stopped playing to yell at him.

"No way!" Stonk chucked his drumsticks at my head. "This doesn't need verses. I hate verses," Stonk growled. "Listen to this." He picked up his drumsticks and started stonking out my **L-L-L-LOSER L-L-L-LOSER** riff while he shouted it out over the beat. His face was twisted up like a demon in a horror film.

Stonk might still be in his room today thrashing out **L-L-L-LOSER L-L-L-LOSER** till his head exploded. But luckily the police showed up after he'd been howling and thumping for twenty minutes. They told me and Stonk to shut up. We almost got ASBOs for making music.

Total

****

After that I thought I'd do better on my own. So I worked on **L-L-L-LOSER** for five days and nights. It was the first time in my life I couldn't think of *anything* else. Forget girl action. Forget pumping up my pecs. I didn't eat. I didn't sleep. I even forgot to shower or look after my face. Think of that! Me? Going to bed without my Nivea night-time cream? Things were bad.

At school I sat in class like a zombie.

No. That's a lie.

I muttered to myself a lot. I kept trying out ideas for words that sounded right. Nothing worked till, all of a sudden, in the middle of a Maths test, this verse for **L-L-L-LOSER** just popped into my head.

"Great stuff," I thought, and jotted it all over my exam paper instead of the sums.

There was a man

He lived alone

On a planet

Of his own

That's crap, I thought when I saw my words written down. I crossed them all out and scrunched my exam paper into a ball. I got kept in after school for that. Plus I got lines when I thought of a tune and sang it out loud in a French lesson.

"**La La Laaaaa. Oh yeah, baby**."

I got even more lines for humming in a high voice while I doodled Ls all over my Art folder.

So that was the week in school when I tried to be a songwriter. Girls who I *know* follow me about because they fancy me, followed me about and giggled at me because I was talking to myself. They elbowed each other and turned away when I sang bits of my song to them. It made me think of how people sniggered at the Two Cheeses when they were at school and bumbled about talking like the hairy Ewoks in *Star Wars*.

But I couldn't help the way I was acting. All I cared about was finishing my song.

Back at home, when I wasn't writing out –

I must not burst out singing in class again unless I sing in French and in tune.

a hundred times, or –

It is not funny when sixteen-year-old boys alarm classmates with nasty humming.

– two hundred times, I kept in my room. Door shut. I didn't even come downstairs to watch telly.

When I look back now, I think, *Idiot! What a waste of telly time!* Those few days were the first time in all my life when I could have had the remote, the sofa and the room to myself.

I could have watched *anything* I wanted – *Kerrang!* VH1. MTV. *SCUZZ* ... In peace. On a telly that wasn't playing non-stop *Star Wars*. In a room that didn't honk of smelly cheese any more. Well, only a tiny bit if you took a deep breath, or sniffed a cushion ...

Because Dane and Lee were ...

Well, that's just it ... I was so into **L-L-L-LOSER L-L-L-LOSER**, so keen to turn it into the best song in the world, I almost didn't notice our house was Dane-free.

Lee-free.

Cheese-free.

I didn't even ask where the Two Cheeses were that week.

Or what they were doing.

"Our Dane's working hard on some project over at Lee's," is all I remember Mum telling my dad, "They've some *Star Wars* doo-dah on Saturday. In London."

I didn't ask my mum what the Two Cheeses' project was. Or what kind of *Star Wars* doo-dah they were going to this time.

Of course I didn't.

I wasn't interested. I just had to finish writing **L-L-L-LOSER L-L-L-LOSER** before it drove me nuts.

But, of course *I* never did finish it ...

Chapter 6
I Want To Be Alone ...

It was Saturday night again. A week since the Two Cheeses had made me so angry that I'd come up with my **L-L-L-LOSER L-L-L-LOSER** chant.

I was still angry. But not with the Two Cheeses any more.

No, I cursed at myself as I walked home in the rain from Frets. I'd had a long day's work and I was dead beat. I was angry with *me*.

I'd spent hours trying to write hot words and a catchy tune to go with my ace hook. What had I come up with?

Nothing.

I'd failed.

Me – John Blue, the rocker.

John Blue, the classy guitar player ...

Who's the ***L-L-L-LOSER*** *now? You are,* I said to myself. I was gutted.

So I crept back into the house. Headed upstairs to my room on tiptoe. I didn't want any "Had a good day?" chat with Mum and Dad. I didn't even feel like eating. I could smell curry – my favourite – but I didn't even care.

"I want to be alone," I said, and I turned my phone off just as it started to ring.

Then I heard it. From the telly room. That bloody tune –

DA **DAH ...** Dadada **DA DAH ...**

How come the *Star Wars* theme was playing when the Two Cheeses were in London?

Were they paying me back for calling them **L-L-L-LOSER L-L-L-LOSER** last week?

Had they set their *Star Wars* DVD to come on just as I came home from Frets?

To tease me?

To haunt me?

"If they've taken the remote to London I'll kill them. Cheesy geeks!" I shouted, and I burst into our sitting room.

"Shut up! Shut up! Shut up!" I growled at the telly, and dived towards it. I was banging all the buttons to make the music stop.

"Oi! Sit down and behave yourself, son," tutted a voice from the sofa. Here was a surprise visitor to the telly room. My dad.

He was parked where Lee always sits. Rather him than me. Dad was waving me away from the screen with a lump of pakora. My mum was sitting next to him.

"Oh, you're home, John. I've been phoning you. Take a plate. Help yourself. And shush," My mum used the remote to point at the carry-out curry on the coffee table. Then she beeped up the volume.

"You're just in time. Guess what? Our Dane's on *Star Wars.*"

Chapter 7
Feel The Force

OK. OK. OK.

Maybe you saw this coming long ago –

The Two Cheeses *had* made it on to *Star Wars with Mr Saturday Night*. Lee must have used the Force. He got through on the phone. Him and Dane were told to come on down to London.

" – and sing to win £10,000," as Jack Gloss was telling the Two Cheeses himself at the start of the show. There they were, Dane and

Lee among all the other contestants. Boy, were *they* looking well out of place. Two geeks in a world of Saturday night bling.

"Let's have a big hand for our stars of *Star Wars* tonight," Jack Gloss told the studio audience as the camera panned the stage.

"Oooh, Dad. Look, there's our big boy. Isn't he handsome?" Mum jumped up and waved at the telly when the camera zoomed in on Dane.

Oooh. Isn't he spotty? I thought to myself.

And why is he wearing a checked shirt of my dad's on a talent show?

And a stupid tie?

And tweedy brown old-man trousers that are too short?

You could see the *Star Wars* socks I bought Dane for a joke last Christmas poking out the bottom.

"Why is Dane dressed like an utter *geek*?" I gasped as the camera panned down and the screen filled with Lee. But I have to say, next to Lee, Dane looked like Brad Pitt! Lee was wearing a dirty-white sweatband round his greasy head and a pair of baggy dungarees. Nothing underneath. I could see one of Lee's bare nipples poking out the side of his denim bib. Yuk! Lee was standing between geeky Dane and dapper Jack Gloss. Picking his nose and eating his bogeys.

I mean Lee was, not Jack Gloss.

I bet glossy Jack Gloss never picks *his* nose, even in private. When he's in his dressing-room with his wig and his make-up off ...

Anyway, right now glossy Jack was too busy shooing all the contestants off-stage to get ready.

"Without further ado," Jack grinned into the camera, "let's welcome the first *fabulous* act tonight. Remember," Glossy Jack twirled his little finger at the screen and his big diamond ring flashed, "THEY sing, **YOU** ring at the end of tonight's show. Vote to make your favourite act a £10,000 winner ..."

Right. Don't panic. I'm only going to give you a mini run-down of the other acts on *Star Wars with Mr Saturday Night*. You're lucky. *I* had to sit through every act and listen to an hour of utter *drivel*.

First up came a flat gospel choir. They forgot the words of 'I Believe I Can Fly'. Half of them fled the stage in tears, tripping on their long gowns. That was quite funny.

But not as funny as **HOney**, a boy band with white suits and even whiter teeth.

Honey made faces like they'd eaten something that had given them the trots and they tried to sing, '*You're Beautiful ...*'

I thought they *were* the trots.

My mum said they were lovely.

But she didn't like the next act.

Ooooh! Not a bit. Four *real* honeys in school uniforms that didn't fit them any more. My dad and I thought *they* were lovely. Not their singing. It was crap, but they did their best with, 'Hit Me Baby, One More Time'. Must have been tricky to sing *and* climb all over each other *and* jiggle about like that. My dad turned down the sound to watch them better.

Then the fourth act minced on dressed up as a mermaid.

"In real life I'm a butcher," the mermaid told Jack, "but tonight I'm Marina and I'm gonna sing 'I Will Survive'."

“You won’t survive long if you sell mince wearing that, mate,” my dad shouted at the telly. When Jack Gloss kissed Marina on the lips, Dad said, “I’m turning this off.”

“Stop! Here’s our boys,” Mum cheered. Just in time she grabbed the remote. Turned the sound up full.

And there was my own brother.

He was on telly. Millions of people were watching. And what was he doing? Showing me up big time, that’s what. He was sitting on a bed wearing *nothing* but all-over spots and a pair of *Star Wars* underpants. Next to him sat Lee. In Han Solo boxers. The wall behind the Two Cheeses was covered with a massive poster of the Millennium Falcon. Dane has Death Star wallpaper so I’m guessing that the Two Cheeses were filmed in Lee’s bedroom.

“Hi. We’re Lee and Dane. We’re eighteen and we come from Glasgow,” the Two Cheeses chanted together. "And when we're not at college being computer students ..." they kept on talking as the TV screen turned all wavy and white as if it was snowing inside the telly.

"We are ..."

DA **DAH ...** Dadada **DA DAH ...**

The *Star Wars* theme tune began as the telly picture went clear again and Dane and Lee chanted, "... Yes. We are THE WORLD'S BIGGEST *STAR WARS* FANS."

Beam me up! No wonder I was peeping through my fingers. There were the Two Cheeses. Still sitting on Lee's bed. Only this time they were all togged up.

Dane as Darth Vader. He was doing his heavy breathing.

Lee as Han Solo. He was flashing his light sabre.

I haven't a clue why the studio audience was cheering two geeks like that. But they were. Jack Gloss was clapping too.

"We all love 'em, don't we?" Jack shouted. "Hey, time to meet these two bright stars on *Star Wars* –" Glossy Jack screeched above the clapping. He was welcoming the Two Cheeses on the stage.

Only he wouldn't know that's what I call them.

Oh, no.

When Jack asked the Two Cheeses, "Who you gonna be tonight, fellas?" they looked into the camera and droned, "Tonight, Jack, we're gonna be 'Feel the Force'. We're gonna do our own song. It's called ..."

Chapter 8
So Bad They're Good

When the Two Cheeses stabbed **L**s on their heads and chanted, "**L-L-L-LOSER L-L-L-LOSER**" at Jack Gloss, I swear I stopped breathing.

My song, I wanted to scream as I heard *my* riff starting up. But I couldn't speak. My mouth was opening and closing like I was a goldfish gasping on the carpet. All I could do was point at the telly. Watch. And listen.

Because the Two Cheeses had started ...

I was going to say "singing". But they didn't sing.

All they did was stand back-to-back, like the Abba girls used to do in their videos. Only the Abba girls never looked ugly or spotty or greasy, did they?

And they used to dance about.

Kinda sexy.

The Two Cheeses didn't move. They kept their arms folded. They glared at the camera. A single note on a keyboard gave them a beat and they chanted words like you'd chant your times tables. Here's what they chanted. Try saying it in a really bored, flat voice.

You look at us and you think we're sad,

'Cos we're not like you and our clothes are bad.

And our hair ain't cool and our breath ain't sweet.

And we've problem skin and we've problem feet.

L-L-L-LOSER!! L-L-L-LOSER!!

You call us –

L-L-L-LOSER!! L-L-L-LOSER!!

'Cos the girls keep back and the phone don't ring,

And we dance like gonks and we just can't sing.

And we're so not buff and we don't work out,

You slag us to our faces. You shout –

L-L-L-LOSER!! L-L-L-LOSER!!

And call us –

L-L-L-LOSER!! L-L-L-LOSER!!

'Cos we stay indoors, watch our DVDs,

You think our life is mi-se-ry.

And you laugh because we never get dates,

And we never go clubbing or drink with our mates.

L-L-L-LOSER!! L-L-L-LOSER!!

You call us –

L-L-L-LOSER!! L-L-L-LOSER!!

You think we're geeks but we just don't care,

About our lack of style or our tragic hair.

Hey, it's you who doesn't have a clue,

'Cos it's us who's here tonight.

Not you!!

L-L-L-LOSER!! L-L-L-LOSER!!

Now who's the –

L-L-L-LOSER!! L-L-L-LOSER!!

So there you have it. The Two Cheeses took my insult. And turned it into a geek rap. A geek rap about me, I suspect.

But do you know what? (And OK, even now it still KILLS me to admit this.) What the Two Cheeses did to **L-L-L-LOSER L-L-L-LOSER** on *Star Wars with Mr Saturday Night* was so bad, it was good.

It was different.

They were different.

The Two Cheeses didn't try to sing like that boy-band **HOney**. Or make faces like they'd got the trots. All the boys bands do that, don't they? And the Two Cheeses didn't jiggle about and spoil their singing like the "Hit Me, Baby!" girls. The Two Cheeses didn't try to be anyone but themselves. They kept still and droned their verses. That meant my **L-L-L-LOSER** chorus really got into your head when they shouted it.

Why couldn't I have thought of something so simple?

By the time the Two Cheeses came to the last **L-L-L-LOSER L-L-L-LOSER** in the song, everyone in the studio audience was making **L** signs and shouting along with the riff.

My riff.

Even glossy Jack Gloss was jabbing an **L** at the Two Cheeses when he came on stage at the end of their act. He was giving them the same sign I'd given them last Saturday night.

Except Jack Gloss chanted, "**W-W-W-WINNER!! W-W-W-WINNER!!**" at Dane. Then Lee.

And the studio audience went wild.

Chapter 9
W-W-W-WINNERS

So. Did Feel the Force win *Star Wars with Mr Saturday Night*?

Oh, come on!

Do Dane's spots look worse under telly lights than they do in real life?

Does Lee look like a giant toddler in dungarees?

Has Jack Gloss had BOTOX?

How can you even *ask* that question?

Of course Feel the Force won!

Their geek rap plus my **L-L-L-LOSER L-L-L-LOSER** riff won Feel the Force over *two million* phone-votes. That was more votes than all the other contestants put together. Plus Dane and Lee landed a b-i-i-i-g juicy cheque ...

I *told* you the Two Cheeses **SHOCKED**!!! me.

But them *winning* wasn't what shocked me the most. It was what they did when Jack Gloss handed them their big juicy cheque at the end of the show.

"So, fellas." Jack slung an arm round each of the Two Cheeses. He pulled them in close to him, flashing his false smile at the camera. Then – I guess – he must have caught a cheesy whiff of what I'm used to smelling, because first his smile, then his arms dropped. Quick-style. He stepped back a bit. He wiped the hand that had touched Lee's shoulder before he winked at the Two Cheeses and asked, "So. What you gonna do with all this money? Fancy a career in show business? Let me tell you, the phones are hot hot hot with record companies wanting to sign you up since we've been on air ..."

"What?"

Back home I was on my feet.

"Show business? Record deals? Hot hot hot?" I was shouting at the telly while my mum and dad told me to, "Shut up or get out!"

Here were the world's biggest geeks being offered *my* dream. On live national television. I'd lick Lee's hair to be in their shoes.

But what did the Two Cheeses do with the offer?

First they gave a shrug. Then they smiled at each other. Shook their heads.

"We're not interested in show business," Dane told glossy Jack Gloss.

"Nah. We like being students," said Lee.

"We like computers," said Dane.

"Yeah. And *Star Wars*," said Lee.

"Yeah. We just came on this show because of *Star Wars*," said Dane.

"And now we're going to use some of our money to go to New York –" Lee nodded at Jack Gloss.

"We'll buy more *Star Wars* outfits," said Dane.

"New action figures. Rare ones," grinned Lee.

"More Lego and Jedi posters and ..."

"Fantastic!" Jack Gloss butted in on Dane. "So you want to hit the big time in the Big Apple?"

"No." Dane shook his head slowly at glossy Jack like he thought glossy Jack was a bit dim. "We want to go to the biggest meeting of *Star Wars* fans –"

"– in the history of the Galaxy!" Lee joined in. The Two Cheeses were punching the air.

"So you don't want to record **L-L-L-LOSER**?" asked glossy Jack. "Pity. You've a hit record here, fellas," he said.

"Oh, right." Lee shrugged. He didn't look one bit bothered. It was as if glossy Jack was telling him he'd got B.O. or zits. "Well," Lee yawned, "a third guy sorta wrote **L-L-L-LOSER** with us. The record companies can talk to him if they like."

"Yeah. Good idea." Dane grinned right into the camera so he looked like he was grinning into my face when he said, "The record companies can talk to my brother. He's called Little Boy Blue."

Chapter 10
Bigger Than Crazy Frog

Get Dane.

Calling me *Little Boy Blue* on national telly.

"Hey, just as well you're in London. Calling me that. You big cheesy geek. 'Cos see, when you get back to Glasgow, you're dead." I was snarling away at our telly when I heard that name again: *Little Boy Blue.* This time glossy Jack Gloss was saying it. Asking the Two Cheeses, "Will you be sharing your prize money with Little Boy Blue?"

"Sure," Dane told Jack. "Me and Lee just needed £500 each for New York."

"Plus spending money," added Lee. "So there's plenty money to share with Little Boy Blue."

"Well, hey, Little Boy Blue, it's your lucky night!" Glossy Jack Gloss grinned right out at me with all his big white teeth as the credits for his show came up over the screen and down his face. Beside him the Two Cheeses waved their hands from side to side in the air as the *Star Wars* theme played.

"Wherever you are, Little Boy Blue, come pick up your phone," Jack Gloss called over the music. "Some people wanna make you a star like Feel the Force ..."

Hmmm.

A star like Feel the Force.

That's the only reason why you'll be reading this story and thinking,

John Blue?

Who?

I've never seen him on CD:UK. *Or* The Chart Show.

What does he look like?

How does his song go?

That's my problem.

See me?

I'm buff. With spot-less skin. I'm a babe-magnet.

Sex on legs. So good, I'm too good.

None of these things I'm saying are me boasting, by the way. It's just what all the record people said when they met me while the Two Geeks were in New York. They told me I was perfect. Then they said, "Er. No, thanks."

They didn't want a cool dude *Pop Idol* guy like me recording **L-L-L-LOSER L-L-L-LOSER**.

"Just wouldn't work, dude. You're too pretty," they told me. They wanted geeks.

No.

Not just any old geeks.

Proper geeks like the Two Cheeses. The real deal – Dane and Lee. In fact the music people wanted the Two Cheeses *so* much, they offered them funny money to record **L-L-L-LOSER L-L-L-LOSER** as a single.

But the Two Cheeses didn't give two hoots. It didn't matter how much money they were offered, their answers were always the same.

"Sorry."

"Not interested."

"Don't wanna be famous."

"We're far too busy."

"With college."

"And the *Star Wars* World Wide Fan Club."

"And going back and forward to the States –"

"To meet up with our girlfriends."

It's all true. Yes, even that line you've just read –

To meet up with our girlfriends.

That's not me making things up or taking the piss out of the Two Cheeses because they wouldn't record **L-L-L-LOSER L-L-L-LOSER**.

It's true. Dane and Lee really did hook up with a couple of ...

Well, they tell me they're two hot New York chicks but, to be honest, I've only seen the Two Cheeses hugging two furry Ewoks in any of the photos they've shown me.

Still, if Ewoks turn the Two Cheeses on, I'm not complaining. Live and let live, I say. It's not like I can grumble about *anything* the Two Cheeses do any more.

For a start I almost never see them.

Dane's moved out. These days him and his spots and Lee live in this big posh house. Every room's done up to make you feel you're in a different *Star Wars* film. It's amazing! And every room smells cheesy. That's disgusting!

But who cares? There's no hint of Dairy Lee or Danish Blue in our telly room at home. There's no telly either. We've a massive plasma screen now. We've put the screen in the new extension I built for my mum and dad. I've turned the telly room into my home recording studio. That's where I compose my ring-tone riffs.

As I say, I can't grumble.

Definitely not about the Two Cheeses.

They might be the world's biggest geeks, but me and my family are set up for life thanks to them ...

Or should I say thanks to them and everyone on the planet who downloaded our **L-L-L-LOSER L-L-L-LOSER** ring-tone onto their mobile phone.

You?

Your mates?

Thanks a million if you have.

No. Really.

Thanks a *million.*

That's what you've made me and the Two Cheeses – millions. And counting.

When the world's biggest phone network bought the rights to **L-L-L-LOSER L-L-L-LOSER** from me and the Two Cheeses, they promised our geek rap would be bigger than Crazy Frog.

And they were spot on.

Barrington Stoke would like to thank all its readers for commenting on the manuscript before publication and in particular:

Elizabeth Baguley
Kate Baguley
Stefan Blanchard
Kathryn Brown
Ella Coultas
Denise Daykin
Martine Ellis
Freya Field-Donovan
Jessica George
Stephanie Grey
Denise Gummer
Harriet Kate Gummer
Anthea Hunter
Madeleine Larke
Marisa Marsh
Harriet Messom
Shafali Miah
Sam Panter
Mandy Riley
Holly Quarterman
James-Ross Webber

Become a Consultant!

Would you like to give us feedback on our titles before they are published? Contact us at the email address below – we'd love to hear from you!

info@barringtonstoke.co.uk
www.barringtonstoke.co.uk

If you loved this book, why don't you try ...

Exit Oz

by Catherine Forde

Meet the star of the show: Oz. My pet corn snake.

How can something SO small cause SO much hassle?

It happened like this: one minute Oz was there, in our hands, and the next ...? Well. He was gone. Exit Oz.

How would we ever get him back?